Bibbidi Bobbidi Academy

Cyrus and the Dragon Disaster

Bibbidi Bobbidi Academy

Cyrus and the Dragon Disaster

Written by Kallie George

Cover illustration and character design by
Lorena Alvarez Gómez

Interior illustrations by Andrea Boatta

Disney · HYPERION

Los Angeles   New York

First Edition, October 2023
1 3 5 7 9 10 8 6 4 2
FAC-073226-23243
Printed in the United States of America

This book is set in Superclarendon, Harman Elegant, Harman Sans/Fontspring.
Designed by Joann Hill
Illustrations created by Andrea Boatta and Lorena Alvarez Gómez

Library of Congress Control Number: 2023941298
Hardcover ISBN 978-1-368-09426-9
Paperback ISBN 978-1-368-09837-3

Reinforced binding for hardcover edition

Visit www.DisneyBooks.com

To Jewell, who loves dragons

–K. G.

Bibbidi Bobbidi Academy

CHAPTER 1

Cyrus Silverstar

Cyrus Silverstar was a star.

A star student at Bibbidi Bobbidi Academy.

That was the school for fairy-godparents-in-training.

But right now, Cyrus didn't feel like a star.

He was high up in the doorway to the Wish Whispering Platform. And he felt scared.

Cyrus was scared of many things.

Like heights. (What if he fell?)

And loud noises. (What could they be?)

Slam!

And big, scary animals. (What if
they growled or snapped at him?)

He could imagine all the
possibilities.

Which was great when he was reading a book.

But not so great when he was thinking of all the things that could go wrong.

Usually, his fears didn't get in his way—much.

But today it was a problem.

For Wish Whispering class, the students were assigned homework.

Each student had to listen for a wish for a pet. Then they had to grant the wish and quickly bring the animal to the Fairy Godmother, their headmistress.

The Fairy Godmother would check the pet's tag and connect the pet with its new owner.

But what if Cyrus got a wish for a big, scary animal?

He wished he were brave like his friends. They weren't afraid of anything. They had all completed the assignment. Except for Rory and Mai, who were on the platform now. They had waited until the last minute to do their homework too. "Bibbidi Bobbidi Boo!"

Poof!

Poof!

"Look, Cyrus!" they said.

Rory and Mai were both holding pets.

"I spelled a cat, and the mat came too," said Rory. Sometimes Rory mixed up her magical spelling. "But the good thing is that now the cat has a bed!" The little cat in her arms mewed.

"Arf," barked Mai's animal, which was mostly fur and fluff.

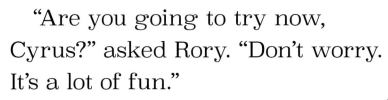

"Are you going to try now, Cyrus?" asked Rory. "Don't worry. It's a lot of fun."

Cyrus took a deep breath and nodded.

After all, his friends had gotten such cute animals.

Surely, he would too.

8

As Rory and Mai left, Cyrus stepped farther onto the platform, making sure not to look over any of the edges.

It was just Cyrus and the early morning sky, still full of stars.

They were big and bright and, if he listened closely . . . buzzing.

Buzzing with the sounds of wishes.

But the wishes themselves were too faint to make out. That's why he needed a Listening Cup.

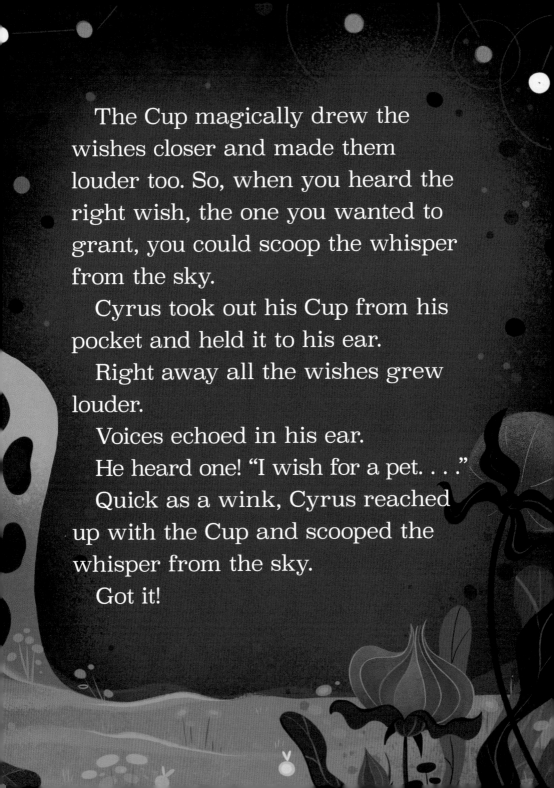

The Cup magically drew the wishes closer and made them louder too. So, when you heard the right wish, the one you wanted to grant, you could scoop the whisper from the sky.

Cyrus took out his Cup from his pocket and held it to his ear.

Right away all the wishes grew louder.

Voices echoed in his ear.

He heard one! "I wish for a pet. . . ."

Quick as a wink, Cyrus reached up with the Cup and scooped the whisper from the sky.

Got it!

The whisper shimmered into the Cup like a firefly.

Quickly, he set the Cup down and took out his wand.

"Bibbidi Bobbidi Boo," he said, before he lost his nerve.

For a moment, the wish swirled around and around in the Cup.

Faster and faster.

Cyrus's heart beat faster and faster too.

He stepped back, just in time.

The Cup spun off the platform and . . .

POOF!

THUD!

UH-OH!

CHAPTER 3
A Darling . . . Dragon?

The pet wasn't a tiny, cute animal.

The pet was a . . . DRAGON!

Cyrus froze.

The dragon was just a baby.

But a baby dragon was still very big.

This baby dragon had bright green eyes, a very pointy tail, and a collar around its neck.

It blinked.

"AHH!" cried Cyrus.

"ROAR!" cried the dragon.

Cyrus stumbled backward and almost dropped his wand.

The dragon lifted its wings.

WHOOSH!

It rose into the air and flew down, down, toward the ground and out of sight.

Cyrus could barely breathe.

A DRAGON?!

His mind raced with his imaginings.

Dragons burned things up with their fiery breath.

They stole treasure with their sharp claws.

They ate everything with their
pointy teeth.

Dragons were *very* scary.
But someone had wished for the
dragon as a pet.

And fairy godfathers granted wishes. Not to mention, this was his homework. What if he didn't finish it? He began to imagine the worst.

Cyrus stopped and took a breath.

He was not brave enough to face the dragon and catch it.

But that was okay. For now.

Because . . . "First things first," he told himself. "I just have to find out where it went."

CHAPTER 4
Homework, Help!

Cyrus stood at the entrance of the Academy. He looked out nervously.

There was no sign of the dragon.

Not in the shadows of the Pumpkin Playground.

Or the glow of the Storybook Shed.

Or in the shimmering Playground Pond, either. Only Ophelia the merfairy was there, having an evening swim.

Then he noticed something. A twist of smoke rose from the Birthday Candle Lab.

That's where students learned about wishing candles.

But the Lab should have been closed at this time of day.

The smoke had to be from the dragon!

Cyrus gulped loudly.

"Are you okay?" came a voice.

Cyrus turned to see Ophelia, poking her head out of the pond. He walked over to her.

"My pet homework got away," said Cyrus. "And it's a dragon," he added, trying not to stammer.

He didn't want Ophelia to know how scared he was.

"A dragon? Wow!" Ophelia gasped. "I've never seen a dragon before. Do you need any help?"

Ophelia loved being helpful.

"Actually, yes," said Cyrus. "Do you know a good water spell? Something to protect me from fire?"

"Do I ever!" Ophelia grinned. "Like this! Bibbidi Bobbidi Boo!" She waved her wand.

SPLASH!

Water soaked Cyrus.

"That was perfect," gasped Cyrus. "Can you show me again?"

"How about I come with you and help?" said Ophelia.

Cyrus didn't protest. Ophelia was so brave, and with Ophelia by his side, he felt a bit braver too.

But not brave enough to face a dragon, so he let Ophelia go first, toward the spiraling smoke.

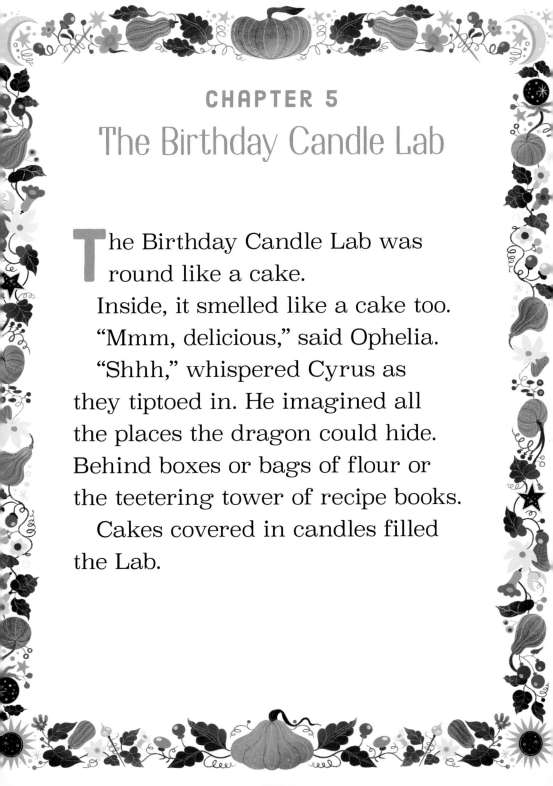

CHAPTER 5
The Birthday Candle Lab

The Birthday Candle Lab was round like a cake.

Inside, it smelled like a cake too.

"Mmm, delicious," said Ophelia.

"Shhh," whispered Cyrus as they tiptoed in. He imagined all the places the dragon could hide. Behind boxes or bags of flour or the teetering tower of recipe books.

Cakes covered in candles filled the Lab.

All kinds and colors. Pink, purple, yellow—even blue.

No, that wasn't a blue cake.

That was the dragon!

Cyrus froze.

The dragon poked its head up from behind a table covered in dishes of sprinkles.

Two tendrils of smoke rose from its nostrils.

It opened its mouth.
"Aahhhh . . ." went the dragon.
"Oh no! Fire!" cried Cyrus.
Ophelia pulled out her wand.

"Bibbidi Bobbidi Boo!" she said.

WHOOSH.

Water sprayed out.
"Aaaa-choo!" sneezed the dragon.
It sent colorful sprinkles, not fire,
into the air.

The water mixed with the sprinkles.
Rainbow rain covered everything!

Cyrus wiped his face and saw the dragon skitter down the hallway.

It reached the candle-shaped chimney, and then . . .

wiggle, wiggle, oomph.

It squeezed up and was gone.

CHAPTER 6
The Tip-Top Leaf

Cyrus and Ophelia raced outside. They were sticky. They were stunned.

They were just in time to see the dragon land on the Tip-Top Leaf.

The Tip-Top Leaf was the highest point of the school. Even higher than the Wish Whispering Platform. It was so high it almost looked like a star.

There was no way Cyrus could fly up there.

To his surprise, Ophelia said, "I am not scared of water, but I *am* scared of heights."

Ophelia was scared too? She always seemed so confident. Like Mai.

That made him remember. . . . "Mai always says the higher the better," said Cyrus. "Maybe she can help us."

They found Mai in her room.

When Cyrus explained, Mai exclaimed, "A dragon! Oh, Cyrus! That's *more* than exciting! And I have just the thing."

She handed him a big bag filled with something sparkly. "To help you fly up high, you need LOTS of pixie dust."

"Do we really need *this* much?" asked Cyrus.

"Even *more*!" said Mai, producing two more bags. "I'll have to come along to carry them. Let's go!"

With Ophelia and Mai along, Cyrus felt a bit braver. But . . . still not brave enough to face the dragon.

When they reached halfway, they sprinkled some of the dust on one another's wings.

Cyrus was still scared, but his wings felt stronger.

Flap, flap, flap.

He imagined himself touching the stars like a fairy astronaut in one of his books.

He could just see the tip of the Tip-Top Leaf. He reached up and grabbed it.

But then . . . the tip of the leaf twitched.

It trembled.

The tip of the leaf was a tail!

"AHH!" cried Cyrus, letting go.

"AHH!" cried Mai and Ophelia.

Whoosh! went the dragon.

Cyrus, Mai, and Ophelia spun
into each other. Their bags burst
open.

Pixie dust filled the air.
When the sparkly cloud cleared,
the dragon was gone—again!

CHAPTER 7
The Cave in the Woods

Now Cyrus was sparkly *and* scared.

There were messes everywhere.

And a child was still left without a wish come true.

Cyrus's homework was a disaster!

But classes hadn't started yet. There was still time.

He took a deep breath.

"Where could the dragon be now?" he said.

"Dragons like fire and flying," mused Mai. "They *also* like treasure."

"Maybe the dragon has gone to the Cave in the Woods," suggested Ophelia. "That's where all the wishing coins are kept."

Cyrus gulped. The cave was deep and dark. But Ophelia was probably right. So, slowly, he nodded.

The cave was at the edge of the woods. Cyrus and Ophelia flew into it together. Good thing Cyrus was a star with a flashlight spell!

Still, it was scary. The shadows left so much room for him to imagine.

"I wish there was more light," Mai whispered. "I am not scared of flying, but I am scared of deep, dark places."

Cyrus couldn't believe it. She was scared too. Just like Ophelia, Mai had fears. Cyrus found Mai's hand and squeezed.

"More light, you said?" came a cackle.

Suddenly there was a glow.

It wasn't from the dragon.

It was Octavia, Ophelia's cousin, with a light coming from her wand.

She was sitting on a pile of glittering coins.

"What are you doing here?" asked Ophelia.

Octavia blushed. Octavia used to be a sea-witch-in-training. But she wanted to be a fairy-godmother-in-training, so she joined the Academy.

"Sometimes I'm a bit overwhelmed by the new school. So I come here to calm down. It is my safe spot. I LOVE treasure."

"I have a safe spot too," said Cyrus. "It's the Storybook Shed."

"Have you seen a dragon?" Mai asked Octavia.

"Dragon?" said Octavia. Her eyes went bright. "No! But I *adoooore* scary dragons! I used to be friends with a sea serpent. What kind of trouble has the dragon caused?"

"Trouble . . . ?" said Cyrus.

"You know. Has it burned anything? Or eaten anyone?"

Cyrus shook his head. The dragon hadn't done anything like that.

But before he could think on this, he heard an echo from far away.

"Dragon! Dragon! There's a dragon in the Pumpkin Playground!"

CHAPTER 8

The Pumpkin Playground

The Pumpkin Playground wasn't far from the Cave in the Woods.

When Cyrus, Ophelia, Mai, and Octavia arrived, they found Tatia and Rory already there.

"We saw a dragon out the window!" said Tatia. "Well, actually *I* saw it first. . . ."

"That's my pet homework," stammered Cyrus. "It escaped."

Everyone started looking for the dragon.

Everyone except Cyrus.

Cyrus felt a bit braver with all his friends there. But still not brave enough to face a dragon!

Usually, the Pumpkin Playground was a fun place.

But right now, it looked scary.

All the play equipment looked like dragons. The Banana Slide looked like a dragon tail.

The Strawberry Swings moved in the wind like dragon wings.

And the Pineapple Play Structure looked like a spiky dragon back.

Cyrus stood, stuck.

Then . . .

"The dragon!" came a shout.

Tatia found it first. The dragon burst out from the Banana Slide. It started to fly.

Soon EVERYONE was flying, frantically trying to catch the dragon.

His friends had faced their fears to help him. Cyrus had to help too.

He tried to remember the heroes in his storybooks. If only he could be half as brave as them.

But he wanted to run away.

Then the dragon opened its mouth.

It was the loudest, *scariest* roar ever.

Cyrus's heart leapt into his throat.

He closed his eyes and flew, as fast as his wings would take him . . . in the complete *opposite* direction.

CHAPTER 9
Being Brave

Cyrus flew and flew until he reached the Storybook Shed.

He landed in a chair and curled into a ball. When the shed wasn't being used for an event, it was a library. It was always open, although the librarian, Ms. Page, wasn't there yet. Storybooks lined the walls.

Stories made Cyrus feel safe.

In stories, if there was a dragon, and you got scared, you could just close the book.

But this was real life. He couldn't close *this* story.

He was definitely not going to catch the dragon.

He was definitely not going to finish his homework.

The wisher wouldn't get their wish.

All because he wasn't brave. Not brave at all. Cyrus sniffled.

Suddenly he heard a sound. Someone else was sniffling too. Someone else was in the Storybook Shed!

Cautiously, Cyrus uncurled and peeked around.

There, in a little corner, Cyrus saw a shadow. The shadow was . . . the dragon!

Cyrus froze. He dared not breathe. He dared not make a sound.

Then . . .

Plip. Plop.

Two big tears slipped down the dragon's snout and fell on the ground.

The dragon wasn't scary.
The dragon was . . .
scared. Scared just
like Cyrus.

All this time, the dragon had just been running away! Maybe the dragon thought *he* was scary.

Oh! Cyrus let out his breath.

But . . . what could Cyrus do?

Cyrus still didn't feel brave enough to face a dragon.

Except maybe you didn't have to feel brave to BE brave.

After all, Mai and Ophelia, and even Octavia, said they were scared sometimes too.

He could imagine all the scary possibilities. But he could also imagine the best ones. Maybe he could even imagine he was brave?

Cyrus took an EXTRA-deep breath.

Slowly, very slowly, he put out his hand and said, "It's okay. I won't hurt you."

The dragon trembled. Cyrus needed something to calm the dragon down.

He needed . . . a story.

Carefully, gently, Cyrus took a book from the shelf. He opened it and began to read.

CHAPTER 10
The Dragon

Cyrus had just discovered the dragon liked funny stories the best when he heard his name being called from outside. "Cyrus!"

The dragon was nestled by his side. He didn't have to catch the dragon at all. The dragon had snuggled by him.

Cyrus wasn't trembling. The dragon wasn't either. Its breath was warm, like the steam from a cup of tea.

Five faces poked into the
Storybook Shed. "Cyrus?"

Their eyes went wide when they saw Cyrus. "Wow! You found the dragon!"

"Shhh!" said Cyrus. "There, there," he said to the dragon. "Just wait here for a moment."

The dragon gave a friendly snort as Cyrus flitted away.

Outside the shed, it wasn't just his friends waiting for him.

The Fairy Godmother and two other teachers, Mr. Frog and Ms. Merryfeather, were there too. It looked like they had all just woken up.

"We heard the clatter. Whatever's the matter?" said the Fairy Godmother, who often spoke in rhyme.

Cyrus was afraid of getting in trouble, but he'd faced so many fears already. One more didn't seem so hard.

Slowly, Cyrus explained everything that had happened. Then he went back into the shed and coaxed the dragon out.

"You need to go to your wisher now," he said gently.

But then he noticed the collar around the dragon's neck was gone!

"Yikes. Your collar must have fallen off."

"Oh no, my dear," said the Fairy Godmother. "If the collar didn't stay, the wisher must have granted the wish another way."

"She found *herself* a pet," said Ms. Merryfeather.

"Oh!" said Cyrus. She had found a way to grant her own wish. Just like he had found a way to be brave, even when he was scared.

He didn't realize he had said this aloud. But he had, because the Fairy Godmother replied, "You know, all us fairy godparents feel scared sometimes."

"You do?" said Cyrus in surprise.

The Fairy Godmother smiled, but her smile wobbled. "Don't get me started on my fear of midnight." She nodded. "So, my dear, your homework is done. Now, off to breakfast, everyone."

"But . . ." stammered Cyrus. "But what about the dragon?"

"Oh, I almost forgot!" The Fairy Godmother gave the dragon a gentle pat.

"It looks like he is happy here. And we don't have a school pet. . . . At least, not *yet*."

"You don't mean . . . ?" said Cyrus.

The Fairy Godmother nodded.

"Of course, we do need to find him a name."

"And someone to help him get used to the school," said Mr. Frog. "It can be scary to adjust to a new home."

"What do you say, Cyrus?" added Ms. Merryfeather.

Cyrus Silverstar couldn't say anything. Not because he was scared. Because he was so happy.

When he found his voice, he said, "I know the perfect name."